STONE SOUP
with
MATZOH BALLS

A Passover Tale in Chelm

Linda Glaser

Illustrated by
Maryam Tabatabaei

www.av2books.com

Your AV² Media Enhanced book gives you a fiction readalong online. Log on to www.av2books.com and enter the unique book code from this page to use your readalong.

AV² Readalong Navigation

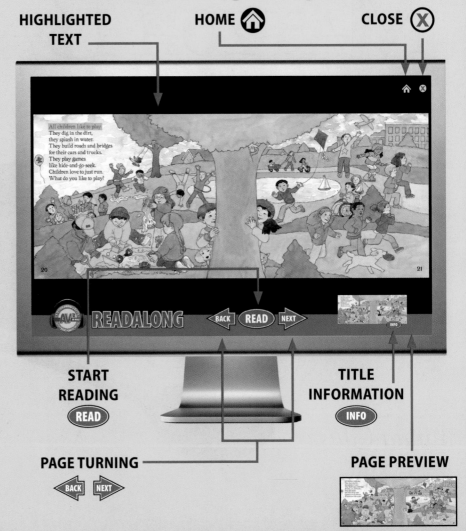

HIGHLIGHTED TEXT

HOME

CLOSE

START READING
READ

PAGE TURNING
BACK NEXT

TITLE INFORMATION
INFO

PAGE PREVIEW

Go to **www.av2books.com**, and enter this book's unique code.

BOOK CODE

U 2 4 6 9 7 5

AV² by Weigl brings you media enhanced books that support active learning.

First Published by

ALBERT WHITMAN & COMPANY
Publishing children's books since 1919

Published by AV² by Weigl
350 5th Avenue, 59th Floor New York, NY 10118
Websites: www.av2books.com   www.weigl.com

Library of Congress Control Number: 2014907235

ISBN 978-1-4896-2416-1 (hardcover)
ISBN 978-1-4896-2417-8 (single user eBook)
ISBN 978-1-4896-2418-5 (multi-user eBook)

Printed in the United States of America in North Mankato, Minnesota
1 2 3 4 5 6 7 8 9 0 18 17 16 15 14

042014
WEP080414

Text copyright ©2014 by Linda Glaser.
Illustrations copyright ©2014 by Albert Whitman & Company.
Published in 2014 by Albert Whitman & Company.

Some people say that Chelm is a village of fools. That may or may not be true. You can decide for yourself. Listen to what happened one Passover when, right before sundown, a poor, ragged stranger arrived and changed the village forever.

"You know what we say at Passover," the stranger proclaimed to the people in the square. "All who are hungry come and eat." He looked around hopefully.

The people of Chelm all looked around too, hoping someone else would invite this hungry stranger in for the Seder.

"We hardly have enough food for ourselves," moaned Faigel.

"It's been such a long winter," groaned Lila.

"Do your belly a favor and go to the next town." Shmuel pointed the way.

Everyone nodded. But the stranger wouldn't budge.

"No food?" He shrugged. "Don't worry!" He pulled a stone from his pocket and held it up. "I can make the most delicious matzoh ball soup with this. All I need is a big cooking pot."

"Impossible!" exclaimed the people of Chelm.
"We're not fools. We know it takes more than a stone to make matzoh ball soup. Everyone knows you also need water!"

So Mendel and Yonkel ran and got the biggest pot,
sloshing full of water.

Meanwhile the stranger made a fire. He placed the pot over the fire and dropped the stone in. Soon the water was boiling.

Yenta peered in. "*Humph!* I don't see any matzoh balls."

"You expect miracles in seconds?" asked the stranger. "First I need a ladle."

So Yenta hurried and got one.

The stranger dipped the ladle into the pot. He poured a little into his cup and took a sip. "*Ahh.*" He rubbed his belly. "For me— a poor stranger—this is delicious. But…" He looked around. "For the good people of Chelm, it could use a little salt."

"No problem." Golda raced home and brought back
a saltshaker in no time.

The stranger sprinkled salt like there was no tomorrow.
He took another sip. "Now this is good enough for a king! But…"
He shook his head. "Not good enough for the people of Chelm.
You don't happen to have any onions in this town?"

"You think we're uncivilized? Of course we have onions!"
Moishe sent the children racing home.

They hurried back with enough onions
to make you cry for a week—maybe two.

Before you could blink, the stranger had a mountain of chopped onions. As he dumped them into the pot, he asked, "Here in Chelm, have you heard of garlic?"

"You think we're fools? Of course we've heard of garlic!"
Zaydel sent the children rushing home again. They hurried back
with enough garlic to choke a horse—maybe two.

The stranger hummed as he dropped the garlic into the pot.
"I suppose carrots are too common for you people of Chelm."

"Too common? *Bah!*" cried Yossel. "Feet are common too. But does that mean we don't use them? Don't be foolish. In Chelm we use our feet and our carrots."

And so it went…
carrots,
celery,
chicken…what a soup!

"*Humph!*" Yenta narrowed her eyes. "Don't think we don't know what you're doing." She shook her finger at the stranger. "What do you mean?" The stranger stopped stirring.

"You said you'd make matzoh ball soup from a stone." Yenta stood on tiptoes so she could glare at him eyeball to eyeball. "You think we're fools?" she cried.

"Of course not," said the stranger.

Yenta put her hands on her hips. "Then where are the matzoh balls?"

"What a wise woman!" said the stranger. "I almost forgot. That stone of mine makes the best matzoh balls in the world—so big and heavy they'll sit in your belly like rocks all eight days of Passover. Guaranteed. You won't need to eat for a week. I'll get them going right now!"

"Wait!" exclaimed Rifka. "Don't you know you're in Chelm? Don't you know we make matzoh balls so light they can almost fly?"

"Impossible!" said the stranger. "I've never met people like you. So wise, so clever. And you can even make matzoh balls?"

"The very best!" The women all hurried home and soon dozens—no, hundreds—of matzoh balls were plopping into the pot.

The soup bubbled away and everyone in Chelm gawked. "Amazing," they exclaimed. "That's some stone."

The rabbi stroked his beard and nodded. "It's a miracle—right before our eyes."

The stranger tried another sip. "*Ahhh!* Now *this* is good enough for the people of Chelm."

It took four men to lug the pot into the synagogue—
the only place where everyone would fit for the Seder.

What a Seder! Plenty of wine and grape juice, piles of matzoh, and enough horseradish to make your toes curl for a year—maybe two.

When it was time for the meal, the stranger stood up.
He clanged the ladle against the soup pot.
"Good people of Chelm! I have something important to say."

A hush filled the room.

The stranger spread his arms wide and proclaimed,
"All who are hungry, please come and eat!"

Some say that the people of Chelm are all fools. But that Passover, everyone had a full belly—even the poor stranger. Now what's so foolish about that?

A Little about Passover

The Jewish holiday of Passover is observed with many rituals including a festive meal called a Seder that takes place at the beginning of the holiday. During the Seder, many traditional foods are eaten such as matzoh (unleavened bread) and matzoh ball soup. At the Seder, the story of Moses leading the Jews from slavery to freedom is read aloud from the Passover book called the Haggadah. A particularly well-known and inspiring line from the Haggadah is "All who are hungry come and eat."

A Little about Chelm

As the story goes, an angel was given a sack of foolish souls to scatter around the world. But the bag got too heavy (or the angel tripped or the bag got caught on a mountaintop, depending on the version), and all the souls spilled out into one small Eastern European village called Chelm. This fictional Jewish town has become a beloved part of Jewish folklore. Stories that take place there—in "the village of fools"—are filled with silliness but also sprinkled with a bit of wisdom. The first stories about Chelm were written in Yiddish in the late 1880s. Since then, Jewish writers have continued to amuse and entertain readers with stories about the "wise people of Chelm" who are famous for coming up with ridiculous solutions to simple everyday problems.

A Little about Stone Soup

The fable of Stone Soup was told in Europe as far back as the 1600s and has since spread to countries around the world. There are many versions but the main idea is always the same. A hungry stranger (or sometimes more than one) comes to town and is turned away from each home until he claims he can make soup from just water and a stone or, in some versions, a nail or an ax or even a button. The people in each area tell it a little differently—including, of course, the wise people of faraway Chelm.

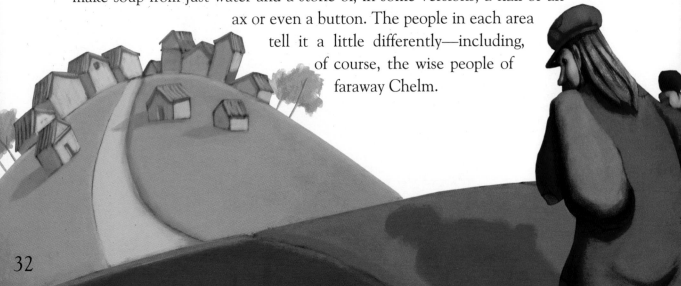